To Market, to Market: Rhymes to Read

To Market, to Market

To market, to market,
  to buy a fat pig;
Home again, home again,
  jiggety jig.

To market, to market,
  to buy a fat hog;
Home again, home again,
  jiggety jog.

Do You Like Apples?

Do you like apples?
Do you like pears?
Do you like falling
  down the stairs?

Do you like white?
Do you like pink?
Do you like falling
  into the sink?

Here We Go

Here we go
up, up, up.

Here we go
down, down, down.

Here we go
forward and backward.

And here we go
round and round.

Three Little Pigs

Three little pigs went to market.
One little pig fell down.
One little pig ran away.
And one little pig
   got to town.

One, Two, Three

One, two, three;
Mother caught a flea.
She put it in the teapot
and made a cup of tea.

Widdy-widdy-wurkey

Widdy-widdy-wurkey
  is the name of my turkey;
There-and-back-again
  is the name of my hen.
Waggle-tail-loose
  is the name of my goose;
Widdy-widdy-wurkey
  is the name of my turkey.

Widdy-widdy-wurkey
   is the name of my turkey;
Quackery-quack
   is the name of my duck.
Grummelty-grig
   is the name of my pig;
Widdy-widdy-wurkey
   is the name of my turkey.

9

Robin

Little Robin Redbreast
sat upon a rail.
Niddle-noddle
went his head.
Wiggle-waggle
went his tail.

Little Bird

I saw a little bird go
hop, hop, hop.
And I said, "Little bird, will you
stop, stop, stop?"

You Can Walk, Walk, Walk

You can walk, walk, walk.
You can talk, talk, talk.
You can eat, eat, eat
with a knife and fork.

The Sausage

I had a little sausage,
a little fat sausage.
I put it in the oven
to eat, eat, eat.

I went to the cupboard
to get the salt and pepper,
and the sausage ran after
my feet, feet, feet.

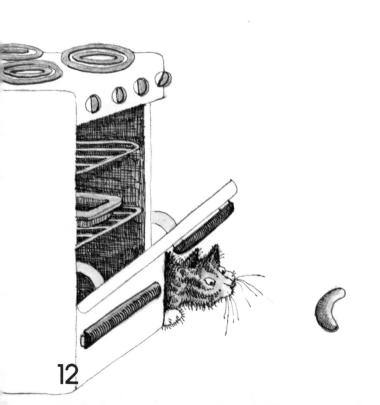

Five Little Pigs

This little pig
went to market.

This little pig
stayed home.

This little pig
had roast beef.

This little pig
had none.

This little pig cried,
"Wee, wee, wee,"
all the way home.

Don't Rain

Rainy, rainy rattlestones,
don't rain on me.
Rain on little Johnny's house
far across the sea.

Rain, Rain

Rain, rain, go away.
Come again some other day.
Little Betsy wants to play.
Rain, rain, go away.

Sally Go Round

Sally go round the stars;
Sally go round the moon.
Sally go round the chimney
on a Sunday afternoon.

On and On

Father and Mother
 and Uncle John
Went to market
 one by one.
Father fell off...
Mother fell off...
But Uncle John
 went on
 and on
 and on
 and on.